La Gran Fiesta

Written and Illustrated by Francisco X. Mora

Highsmith
P R E S S

Fort Atkinson, Wisconsin

Published by Highsmith Press
W5527 Highway 106
P.O. Box 800
Fort Atkinson, Wisconsin 53538-0800

The paper used in this publication meets the minimum requirements of American National Standard for
Information Science - Permanence of Paper for Printed Library Material. ANSI/NISO Z39.48-1984

About the Author

Francisco Mora was born in Mexico City in 1952, where he studied traditional and contemporary art with some
of Mexico's most influential artists. Later he continued his studies in Europe and the United States. With bright
colors, mythical creatures and Mexican folklore, he creates a whimsical world of fantasy that subtly teaches about
reality. His writing and illustrations are interpretations of his dreams, memories and past, which draw heavily on
his childhood recollections of the sights, sounds and flavor of his Mexican heritage.

Library of Congress Cataloging-in-Publication Data

Mora, Francisco X.
    La gran fiesta / written and illustrated by Francisco
X. Mora.
      p. cm.
    Summary: Relates how Crow and his friends taught
everyone to celebrate Christmas.
     ISBN 0-917846-19-2 (alk. paper) : $19.00
     [1. Birds--Fiction. 2. Christmas--Fiction.] I. Title
PZ7.M788185Gr   1993
[E]--dc20   92-44365
                                    CIP

One day Crow flew down to sit on the highest branch of the Little Tree.

Crow was so big and heavy that when he landed the poor Little Tree shook all over.

Hundreds of Little Birds awoke to the shaking of the tree.
"What is going on?" they chirped. "Is this an earthquake?"

"It's only me," said Crow. "Forgive me for disturbing you so early, but there is something very important that you all should know."

The Little Birds quieted down to listen.

The Little Birds respected Crow. He was big and tall, elegantly dressed in black. But they all knew he was a trickster from time to time.

"*La Gran Fiesta de Navidad* is coming," he announced. And I have decided this year to use the Northern tradition of decorating a tree.

"A tree? What kind of tree?" the Little Birds asked.

"We shall use the tallest tree in *el bosque*. And as it is happens to be mine, I have decided to lend it to be used for *La Gran Fiesta*," Crow said.

Even though they were very suspicious of
Crow's idea, they agreed to help decorate the
tree. Crow couldn't be THAT bad.

"How shall we decorate the tree?" the Little
Birds asked.

"*Flores* y *frutas* shall decorate our tree!" Crow declared.

"*Dulces* y *galletas* would make tasty decorations," he
thought to himself.

The Little Birds were excited.

"Start bringing those goodies of *dulces* y *frutas* to my tree,…I mean, our
tree. There are only a few days left until *La Gran Fiesta de Navidad*.

After all the Little Birds had flown away to gather treats for the tree, Crow said to himself, "Now I won't have to worry. I will have food throughout the winter and those foolish Little Birds will bring it to me!"

He laughed and flew back to his tree to wait.

One by one the Little Birds brought decorations for the tree.

They brought *charamuscas, alegrías, chocolates, y pepitorias.*

They brought *guavas, mangos, cerezas, nanches, y chirimoyas,* too!

The Little Birds even brought flowers of *noche buenas, alcatraces, y azaleas* to decorate the tree!

It was almost sundown on the eve of *La Gran Fiesta* when Crow was hanging the last decorations on the beautiful tree. There were now so many *dulces* y *frutas* that the branches began to bend.

Still, Crow insisted upon hanging one more *charamusca* on the tree.

Isn't this the best tree ever? Isn't it wonderful?" he asked the Little
Birds as he admired the tree.

Crow flew to the top of the tree, perching himself on the highest
branch.

"Be careful, don't sit on that branch," the Little Birds warned.

Crow only had time to look down at them, when a loud *CRAC!* invaded the tranquil forest.

The Little Birds scattered in all directions as the tree collapsed.

After the crash, the Little Birds found Crow lying in the middle of a pile of fruit and candy.

"You silly Birds! See what you have done! I told you not to bring so many decorations. Now the tree is broken and the goodies are ruined. And look at my feathers! They're all dirty. You'd better start cleaning up this mess right away!" Crow said angrily.

The Little Birds were surprised, but they apologized to Crow. They knew the tree was ruined because of Crow's greediness.

"Maybe some things can still be saved in time," said the Little Birds hopefully. "What is most important, we have each other to enjoy."

"Oh sure," Crow pouted. "But now we must have *La Gran Fiesta de Navidad* without a beautiful tree.

The Little Birds began to gather fallen fruits and candies for *La Gran Fiesta*. Not wanting to leave Crow alone, they invited him to join them.

As they worked, the moon appeared in the night sky and placed itself at the top of the Little Birds tree. Hundreds of stars joined the moon, flying to each branch, like tiny lights decorating its branches. The stars twinkled and the moon glowed at the top.

The Little Tree was beautiful!

The Little Birds were very grateful for the wonderful gift. The moon and stars had decorated their tree.

"*La Gran Fiesta* is a success after all!" chirped the Little Birds

"Best of all, there's plenty of time for me to find a new tree to decorate for next year's *Gran Fiesta*!" laughed Crow.

Glossary of Spanish Words

La Gran Fiesta
The Big Party

alcatraces   (al ca tráh ses)
cala lilly

alegría   (a lay grée ah)
happiness (candy made of
amaranth seed and honey)

azalea   (a sáy lee ah)
azalea (flower popular in Mexico)

bosque   (bóse keh)
forest (also in reference to a rain
forest)

cereza   (ser ráy suh)
cherry

charamusca   (char ra móose ka)
twisted carmel candy

chirimoya   (chir ree móy a)
sour sop fruit (also from Puerto
Rico)

chocolate   (cho co láh tay)
chocolate (originating from
cacahuetl, an Aztec word, for a
popular beverage)

dulce   (dóol say)
candy

flores   (flóor ays)
flowers

fruta   (fróo tah)
fruit

galleta   (guy yét tah)
cookie

guayaba   (gwah yá ba)
guava (tropical fruit)

mango   (máhn go)
mango (tropical fruit)

manzana (mahn sá nah)
apple

nanche (nán chay)
nanche (tart yellow berry from
Mexico

naranja (nah rán ha)
orange

Navidad (Nah vee dáhd)
Christmas

noche buena (nó chay bwáy na)
poinsettia (flower originally
grown in Mexico)

pepitoria   (pep pee tor ée ah)
candy (wafers of pumpkin seed
and honey)